Why in the World?

Why Isn't Pluto a Planet?

A Book about Planets

by Steve Kortenkamp

Consultant:
James Gerard
Aerospace Education Specialist
Kennedy Space Center

Mankato, Minnesota

First Facts is published by Capstone Press,
151 Good Counsel Drive, P.O. Box 669, Mankato, Minnesota 56002.
www.capstonepress.com

Printed in the United States of America

Library of Congress Cataloging-in-Publication Data
Kortenkamp, Steve.
Why isn't pluto a planet?: a book about planets / by Steve Kortenkamp.
p. cm.—(First facts. Why in the world?)
Summary: "A brief description of planets, including what they are, where they are, and how they orbit around the sun"—Provided by publisher.
Includes bibliographical references and index.
ISBN-13: 978-0-7368-6753-5 (hardcover)
ISBN-10: 0-7368-6753-8 (hardcover)
1. Pluto (Planet)—Juvenile literature. 2. Planets—Juvenile literature. 3. Solar system—Juvenile literature. I. Title.
QB701.K57 2007
523.4—dc22 2006025648

Editorial Credits
Megan Schoeneberger, editor; Juliette Peters, set designer; Renée Doyle, book designer; Wanda Winch, photo researcher/photo editor

Photo Credits
Calvin J. Hamilton, 10, 16–17 (inset)
NASA/ESA and A. Feild (STScI), 20; ESA, S. Beckwith (STScl) and the HUDF Team, 18; JPL, 6 (top middle, bottom middle, bottom right), 9, 12–13, 16–17 (main photo); JPL, U.S.G.S., 6 (middle right); JSC/Pat Rawlings (SAIC), 21
Peter Arnold/Astrofoto, 4
Photodisc, cover (Saturn), 6 (top left, top right, middle left, bottom left), 8
Shutterstock/Fred Goldstein, 5
SuperStock/Mauritius, cover (Pluto)

1 2 3 4 5 6 12 11 10 09 08 07

Table of Contents

What Is a Planet?

Millions of space objects orbit our Sun, yet only eight of them are planets. What makes them so special? First, they are all round. Secondly, they don't have any other objects their size floating nearby. That's what makes them planets.

Scientific Inquiry

Asking questions and making observations like the ones in this book are how scientists begin their research. They follow a process known as scientific inquiry.

Ask a Question

Can I see the planets without a telescope?

Investigate

Go out each night just after sunset and carefully draw a picture in a notebook of the stars you see in the western part of the sky. Record the date and time that you draw each picture. Be patient. You may have to draw pictures over several weeks.

Explain

Most of the stars in your pictures stay in the same pattern. Look for one star that moves in the pattern. That wandering object isn't a star at all. It's a planet. Record your findings in your notebook. It could be a new discovery!

Mercury
Venus
Earth
Mars
Jupiter
Saturn
Uranus
Neptune

What Are the Eight Planets Like?

Earth is the easiest planet to see and explore. You're on it! Mercury, Venus, and Mars are other rocky planets like Earth. Jupiter, Saturn, Uranus, and Neptune are giant gas planets.

Here's one way to remember the planets in order from the Sun: My Very Excellent Mother Just Served Us Noodles. Or try making up your own sentence!

Like people, each planet is different in some way. Most of them have an **atmosphere**. But not Mercury. Jupiter, Saturn, Uranus, and Neptune have **rings** of dust, ice, and rocks. The others do not.

A planet doesn't need to have a moon. Mercury and Venus don't have one. Jupiter has more than 60 moons.

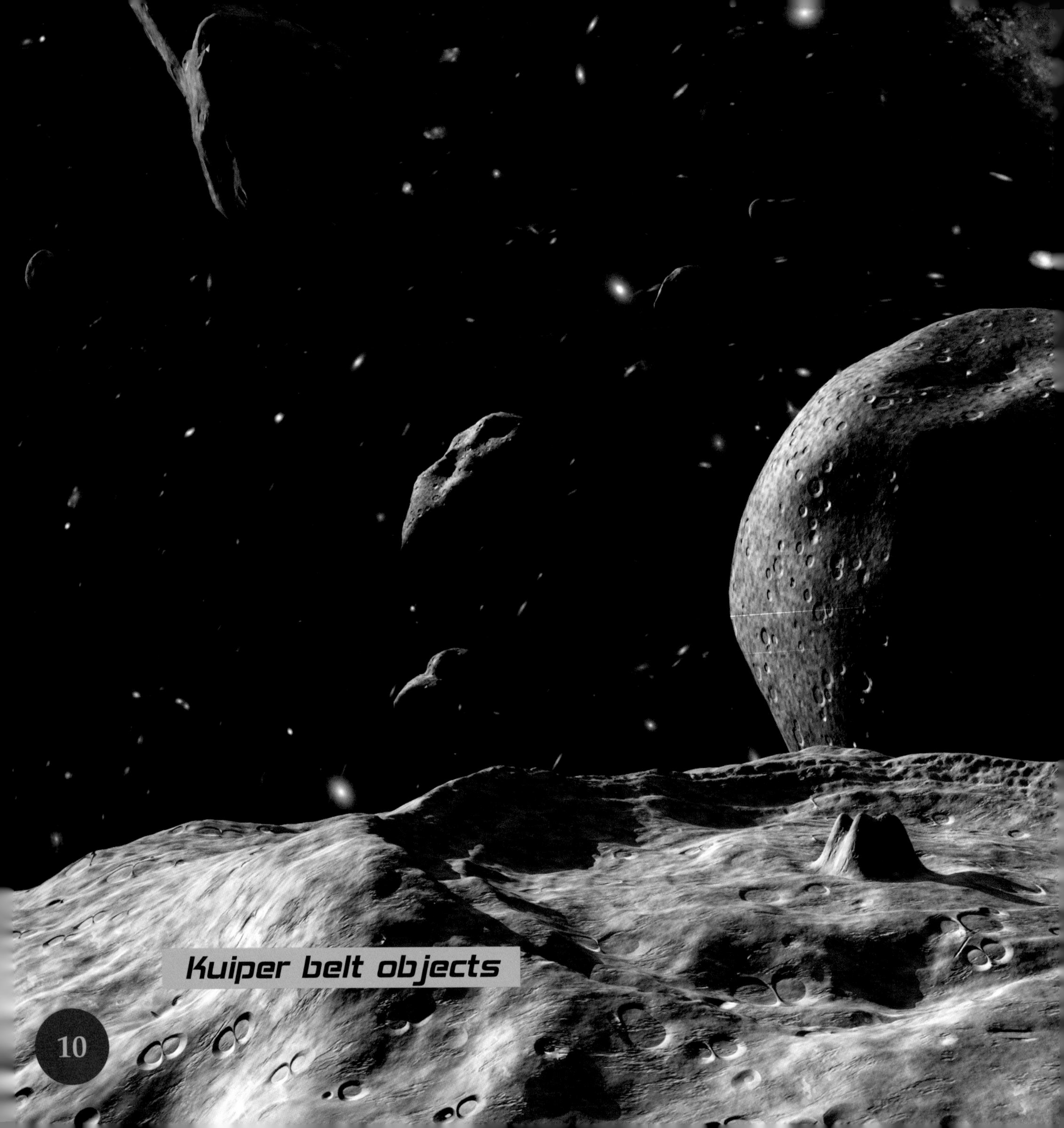

Kuiper belt objects

Why Isn't Pluto a Planet?

For more than 75 years, Pluto was called the ninth planet. But in 2006, astronomers decided a planet needed to be the only large object in its area. Pluto shares its space with hundreds of other objects. Some of them are as big as or bigger than Pluto. That's why Pluto isn't called a planet anymore.

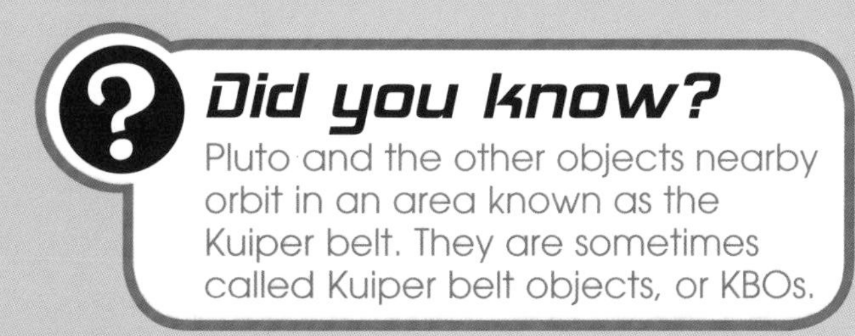

How Big Is the Solar System?

Very big. Imagine shrinking the solar system down until Earth is the size of a grape. Saturn would be 10 city blocks away. Uranus would be 20 blocks away.

It takes a spacecraft about six months to reach Mars. Think that's long? Saturn is seven years away!

Did you know?

If Earth were the size of a grape, Jupiter would be the size of a grapefruit. Saturn would be an orange. Uranus and Neptune would be lemons.

Cassini spacecraft orbiting Saturn

Orbits

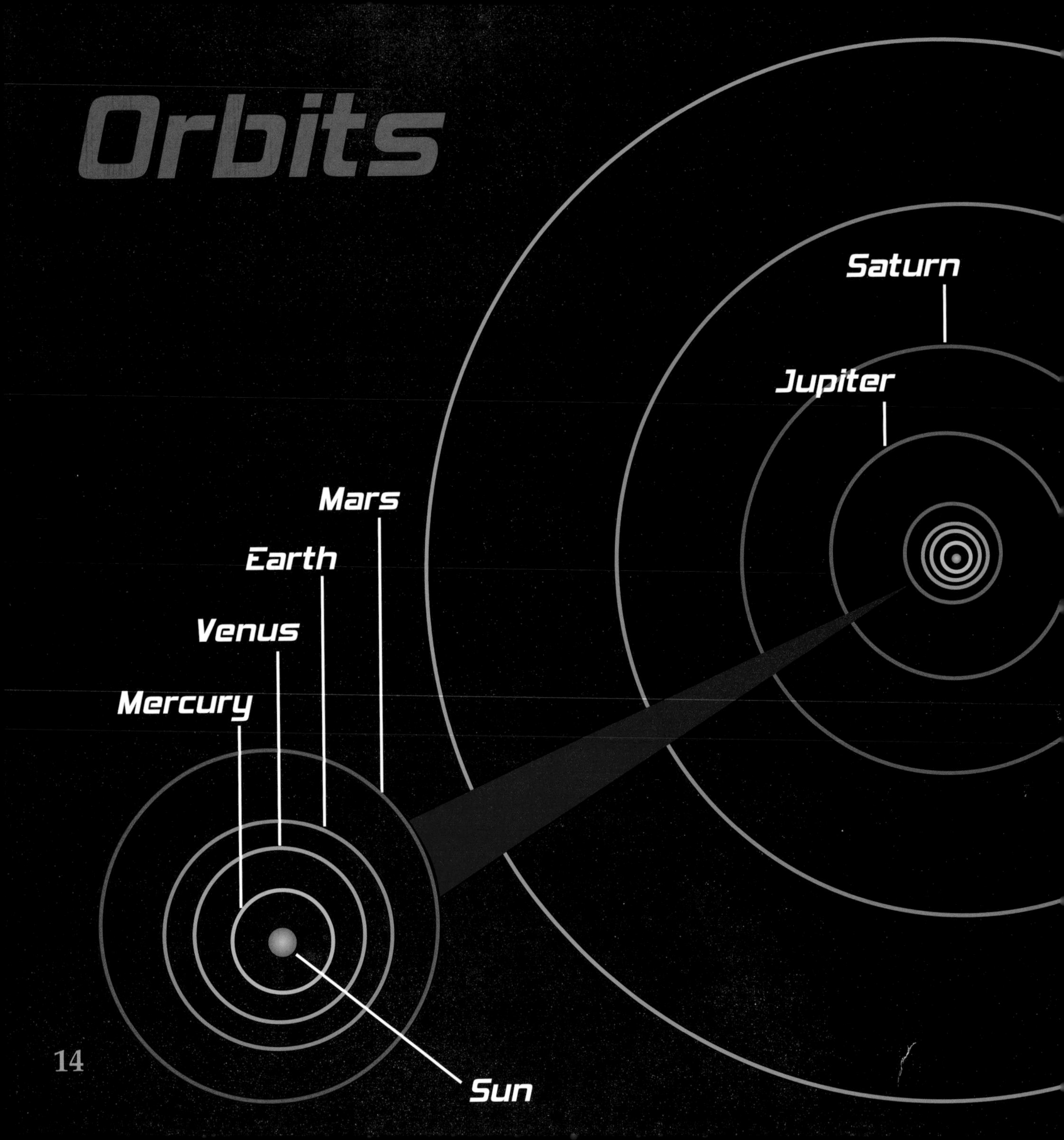

Neptune
Uranus

Do Planets Have Years Like We Do on Earth?

For all planets, one year equals one trip around the Sun. Years are measured by how many days on Earth it takes to make the trip.

One year on Earth lasts 365 days. Mercury whizzes around the Sun in 88 days. Neptune needs 60,190 days, or about 165 Earth years.

How Long Is a Day on Mars?

Planets also **rotate** like spinning tops around an imaginary line called an **axis**. Rotation makes the sun appear to rise and set in the sky. One full day is from sunrise to sunrise. On Earth and Mars, days are about 24 hours long. But on Venus, days drag on for about 2,802 hours.

sunrise on Mars

nearly 10,000 galaxies as seen from the Hubble Space Telescope

Are There Any More Planets?

Our Sun is just one of billions of stars in the Milky Way **galaxy**. With telescopes, astronomers have found planets orbiting hundreds of those stars. Billions of other galaxies make up the universe. Each galaxy has billions of stars. Imagine how many other planets must be out there!

CAN YOU BELIEVE IT?

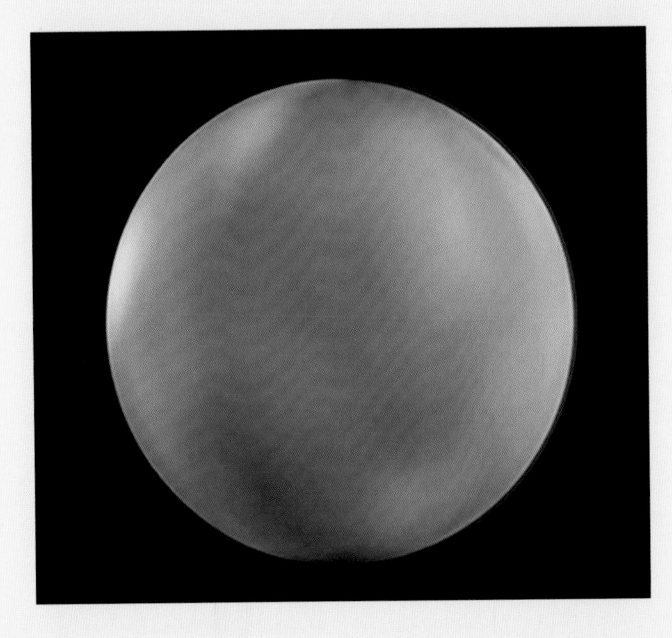

In 1801, astronomers spotted Ceres in the sky and called it a planet. But they soon found more rocky objects nearby. They decided Ceres was not a planet. In 2006, astronomers thought about making Ceres a planet again. Instead, they decided to call it a dwarf planet like Pluto.

WHAT DO YOU THINK?

Besides Earth, some scientists think Mars is the most likely planet in our solar system to support life. They have sent robots to Mars to look for signs of life. One thing they look for is water. What else do you think life would need to survive on another planet?

GLOSSARY

atmosphere (AT-muhss-feehr)—the mixture of gases that surrounds some planets and moons

axis (AK-siss)—an imaginary line that runs through the middle of a planet; a planet spins on its axis.

galaxy (GAL-uhk-see)—a very large group of stars and planets

moon (MOON)—an object that moves around a bigger object in space

orbit (OR-bit)—to travel around a planet, the Sun, or any other object in space; the path an object follows while circling another object in space is also called an orbit.

ring (RING)—a band of ice, rocks, and dust orbiting a planet

rotate (ROH-tate)—to spin around; Earth rotates once every 24 hours.

READ MORE

Croswell, Ken. *Ten Worlds: Everything That Orbits the Sun.* Honesdale, Penn.: Boyds Mills Press, 2006.

Olien, Rebecca. *Exploring the Planets in Our Solar System.* Objects in the Sky. New York: PowerKids Press, 2007.

Sparrow, Giles. *Planets and Moons.* Secrets of the Universe. Milwaukee: World Almanac Library, 2007.

INTERNET SITES

FactHound offers a safe, fun way to find Internet sites related to this book. All of the sites on FactHound have been researched by our staff.

Here's how:

1. Visit *www.facthound.com*
2. Choose your grade level.
3. Type in this book ID **0736867538** for age-appropriate sites. You may also browse subjects by clicking on letters, or by clicking on pictures and words.
4. Click on the **Fetch It** button.

FactHound will fetch the best sites for you!

INDEX